KANGA ROO

RABBIT

OWL

CHRISTOPHER ROBIN

Eeyore
AND THE
Balloon Tree

by Ronald Kidd
illustrated by Vaccaro Associates, Inc.

Based on the Pooh stories by A.A. Milne [copyright the Pooh Properties Trust].

Edited by Ruth Lerner Perle
Produced by Graymont Enterprises, Inc.
Design and Art Direction by Michele Italiano-Perla
Pencil Layouts by Ennis McNulty
Painted by Lou Paleno

ISBN 0-7172-8443-3

Printed in the United States of America.

Grolier Books is a Division of Grolier Enterprises, Inc.

Spring had come to the Hundred-Acre Wood. The sun was shining, the bees were buzzing, and Winnie the Pooh was walking in the forest.

Pooh hummed a little hum as he walked, thinking what a fine thing it was to be a bear in the spring.

Not far away, at the edge of a pond, Eeyore was practicing his smile. First he raised one corner of his mouth. Then he raised the other. Somehow, he couldn't keep them both up at once.

As Eeyore stared at his reflection, a smiling face appeared beside him. It was Winnie the Pooh.

"How do you do it, Pooh?" asked Eeyore.

"Well," said Pooh, "the important thing is . . . and of course, one should always be careful to . . . " Pooh sighed and asked, "How do I do what, Eeyore?"

"Oh, nothing," Eeyore replied still trying to smile.

"Nothing?" said Pooh. "Why that's easy. First you need a jar of honey. Which reminds me . . . oh, bother, I was supposed to tell you something."

"It couldn't have been very important," Eeyore said.

"But it *was* important!" Pooh said. "It had to do with honey, and—I know! There's a picnic to celebrate Spring, and we're all invited."

"Come on, it will be fun!" said Pooh.

"Fun?" Eeyore replied. "I don't know how much more fun I could stand."

Pooh set off through the forest. Eeyore, curious to see how much more fun he could stand, followed behind.

Soon they came to a meadow, where Christopher Robin had spread out a blanket. On the blanket were Piglet, Rabbit, Owl, Tigger, Kanga, and little Roo.

"Everyone is here now," said Roo. "Let's eat!"

Christopher Robin opened his picnic basket. He pulled out treats for everyone, including a jar of honey for Pooh.

"I could do with just a little taste of that," said Pooh, "after the long, honeyless walk I just had."

Christopher Robin pulled a lovely bunch of thistles
from the basket.

"Really," Eeyore said glumly, "you needn't have brought
anything for me."

"Then who will eat these?"
Christopher Robin asked.

"Well, I suppose I could," said
Eeyore. "I hate to see good thistles
go to waste."

After lunch, Christopher Robin said, "And now I have a special surprise." He reached into the basket and brought out a handful of little brightly colored droopy things.

"What a wonderful surprise," said Eeyore sadly. "Little droopy things."

"Silly!" said Rabbit. "They're balloons."

Eeyore replied, "Excuse me, but I'm quite sure balloons have more of a rounded shape."

"Just wait and see," said Christopher Robin with a smile. Eeyore watched as Christopher Robin put one of the little droopy things to his lips and blew into it until it was a bouncy round balloon. Then he tied a string to it and gave it to Rabbit.

Christopher Robin kept blowing up more colorful balloons and gave each one to his friends.

The last little droopy thing was red. "This one is for you, Eeyore," said Christopher Robin. He blew until the red balloon was big and shiny.

Then everybody went running through the meadow, the balloons bobbing behind them like happy thoughts.

As Eeyore trotted along behind the others, he suddenly heard a loud POP! Eeyore looked up at the tree above him. There, hanging from a branch, was a small piece of red rubber that used to be his balloon.

Eeyore pulled the string, and the piece of balloon fell to the ground. He picked it up and gazed at it sadly.

"Oh, well," he sighed. "I always was fond of little droopy things."

12

Eeyore sat down beneath the tree and sang a sad song.

Spring is great if your first name is Tigger,
And it's fine if your last name is Pooh.
But if Eeyore's your name, though you're not to blame,
Spring simply isn't for you.

For some, daisies bloom in the meadow,
And big balloons float in the sky.
But for Eeyores and such, thanks very much,
Spring is hopeless. I don't know why.

When Eeyore finished singing, Owl said, "See here, Eeyore, there's more to spring than just balloons." He tried to explain about bees buzzing and flowers blooming, but somehow he always seemed to end up talking about his great-uncle Timothy.

" . . . and Timothy," said Owl, "was an expert on customs around the world."

This sounded quite interesting to Pooh, especially the part about custards around the world. He wanted to ask about them, but by the time Owl stopped to take a breath, Pooh had forgotten the question.

The next day, to cheer up Eeyore, Pooh took him for a walk through the forest. Everywhere they went, they saw their friends planting.

Kanga and Roo were planting ivy in their window boxes so that Roo could see the vines climb around the window.

Piglet was planting haycorns in his yard, so he'd never have a shortage of haycorn pies.

HAYCORN SEEDS

16

And Rabbit was planting vegetable seeds in his garden so he could bake lots of carrot cakes.

17

Pooh and Eeyore stopped to watch Rabbit work.

"Rabbit," said Pooh, "would you mind showing us how to do it? Planting, I mean."

"To begin with, you must have seeds," said Rabbit.

Pooh looked all around the garden and said, "But, Rabbit, could you tell us, what exactly is a seed?"

"A seed is a special, small part of a plant," Rabbit said. "You put it in the ground, water it, and weed it as it grows. Most important, you keep Tiggers from bouncing on it."

"Planting sounds like a lot of work," said Eeyore.

"Oh, but it's worth it!" Rabbit said. "Especially if you're planting something you like and want more of — carrots, for instance."

18

19

Eeyore tried to think of something he wanted more of. That was when he got his Wonderful Idea.

"Pardon me," he said, "but I believe there's something I need to do."

Eeyore went into the forest and got something he wanted more of. He took it home to his gloomy place. There he dug a hole in the ground. He put the piece of balloon he had been saving into the hole and covered it up.

Eeyore had planted a balloon tree!

Every morning, Eeyore watered the soil and weeded it just as Rabbit had instructed. Then he sat back and dreamed of the day when his balloon tree would be tall and beautiful, with colorful balloons hanging from every branch.

.22

After a few weeks, Piglet's haycorns
sprouted.

Kanga's ivy curled down the side of the
house and out across her yard.

The green tops of Rabbit's vegetables
peeked out above the ground. Everything
was growing—well, almost everything.

Eeyore sat staring at the ground, watching for signs of a balloon tree. Seeing none, he shook his head sadly.

"Well, what can one expect?" he sighed.

"Pardon me, Eeyore," said Pooh as he came wandering by. "But what are you looking at?"

"I'm looking at my balloon tree," Eeyore said. "How do you like it?"

Pooh inspected the ground and said, "It's really quite nice, though not as balloonish as most, don't you think?"

Eeyore told Pooh about his Wonderful Idea—how he
had planted a small part of the balloon, and how he had
watered and weeded it every day. He had even stood
watch to make sure it was safe from Tigger bounces. But
despite all his hard work, there was no balloon tree.

Pooh was sorry to see Eeyore so sad, but being a bear
of very little brain, he didn't know what to do. So he
hurried off to see Christopher Robin.

The next day, as usual, Eeyore trudged out of the forest and into the meadow to see if his tree had started to sprout.

There, growing straight up out of the ground, was a balloon tree! It wasn't as tall as he had hoped. In fact, it was quite small. But there were brightly colored balloons hanging from every branch.

28

As Eeyore gazed at the tree, Winnie the Pooh stepped out of the forest, holding Christopher Robin's hand. With them were Piglet, Owl, Tigger, Rabbit, Kanga, and Roo.

"Well, everybody, how do you like my balloon tree?" Eeyore asked proudly.

"Eeyore," Christopher Robin said gently, "this is not really a balloon tree. But it is a very *special* tree, planted and decorated with balloons by your friends."

"I should have known," Eeyore said sadly. "I can't even grow a balloon tree."

"But this will grow, Eeyore," said Christopher Robin. "Tell him, Pooh."

"That's right, Eeyore," said Pooh Bear. "It's a friendship tree that will blossom every year to remind you of all your friends who love you."

Suddenly, Eeyore felt something odd happening to his mouth. One side went up and stayed there. Then the other side began twitching in an upward direction. Up, up, up it went, as if tugged by a balloon.

Eeyore was finally smiling!